TEASED BY MY ROOMMATE

HALEY TRAVIS

1

LILA

As I placed my key in the first lock, I could feel the familiar Friday evening energy wash over me. Then the second lock clicked open, and I leaned against the heavy door to my new home and pushed.

Peace and quiet in my strange apartment.

Walking through the giant warehouse loft space, I dropped my bag on a kitchen chair and headed straight for the coffee maker. Half-caff hazelnut with a touch of whipped cream was going to be my exciting start to the weekend.

Just as I finished filling the pot, I heard the shower start. Perfect timing, since I'd heard the water pressure was sketchy in this ancient building.

Checking the calendar on the fridge, it looked like Ashley was supposed to have gone home this morning. She must have stayed an extra day, since there was herbal tea still stashed on the shelf. She was only here for a few days around twice a month, when her company sent her to conferences and training programs in the city. She hated hotels, and the monthly rent was so cheap here that it was more affordable.

It seemed that Ashley was popping by more often, though, as if it were worth the long drive to have some alone time. I completely got that.

I'd been looking forward to an evening totally by myself, but oh well. I'd likely have the rest of the weekend for that. Brooke, our third roommate, had moved out last week after suddenly switching schools, but apparently her cousin was going to be subletting her room.

Six months ago I would never have believed I'd be living with strangers, but it was worth it to be free of my family.

I rummaged in the fridge, but the leftover chicken and rice I'd been looking forward to for dinner was gone. Then I noticed the empty bowl was on the counter, unwashed.

Sigh.

I popped into my room to change, slipping into thread-bare yoga pants and a long, stretched out tank top. I was glad to get out of my bra and work pants. Since it was just us girls, I let my hair down for good measure, and threw on a zip up hoodie.

The coffee finished brewing, and I was just preparing two mugs with plenty of whipped cream when I heard the shower shut off. The bathroom door opened, and I turned with a mug in my hand, expecting to see Ashley in her light pink robe.

Then my mouth fell open with a pitiful, nearly desperate sound.

A tall, beautifully muscular man walked out while drying his hair with a towel.

He was not wearing anything else. Well, unless you counted the water droplets sparkling across his chest.

My eyes gravitated lower, drinking in his perfectly toned, strong body, including—

Oh my.

Dazzling brown eyes met mine as I snapped my gaze back to his face. He'd caught me staring at his...

I swear it twitched and started to thicken.

Chuckling, he lowered the towel to cover his groin. "Most girls usually buy me flowers if they want a peep show, but I'll take that coffee if it's for me."

Somehow my feet moved forward as he approached me. His luscious torso...those sculpted lines over his hips...every other delicious part of his body...it was all still on full display.

A huge tattoo of a hawk took up most of his right arm, and the left one was completely covered in what looked like Celtic scrollwork. I'd never thought about how sexy muscled thighs were, but then, I'd never seen a naked man in person before.

"Thanks," he said, taking the mug from my shaking hand. He sipped it carefully, then licked the whipped cream from his top lip. It was the most seductive gesture I'd ever seen.

"It's nice to meet you, Lila."

"Um, who are you?" I stammered.

"Brooke's cousin." He set the mug on the table, then turned away to wrap the towel low around his hips, drawing more attention to those perfect V-lines. Then he reached out to shake my trembling hand. "Hawk."

Closing my eyes for a second, all I could picture was something long and thick that rhymed with his name.

"Hi. Nice to meet you too."

His hand held mine for much longer than necessary.

The way his eyes dragged down my chest, clearly admiring my body, made me tingly inside.

"Let me guess. Brooke didn't tell you that her cousin was a guy?"

"No. She was so busy she didn't even say when you were moving in."

"Surprise, I guess. That was this morning." He released my hand, picking up his mug. "Why don't we get to know each other over dinner?"

"Sure. I had some leftovers, but they're gone."

Hawk smiled sheepishly. "Yeah. Sorry about that. I was ravenous after the drive and hauling my stuff up the stairs. Then I had to go buy a bigger bed."

All three rooms had identical single beds, and yeah, there was no way Hawk could fit.

"Let me order us dinner," he said before taking another sip of coffee. Then he grinned. "This is amazing. I don't normally go for the sugary stuff, but..." He trailed off, letting his eyes run up and down my figure again. "I think I'm in the mood for something sweet tonight."

Was he hitting on me? No, he couldn't be. No man ever hit on me, for fear that my family might—

Oh. That's right. He had no idea who I was.

For the first time ever, that wasn't an issue.

Hawk was teasing me as if I were any other normal girl. Maybe he wouldn't treat me as spoiled or precious, or someone risky to be avoided. This seemed like an incredible step forward, if I could find a way to actually speak around a man that gorgeous.

"Sounds great," I said. Two words. It was a start.

Grabbing my phone and coffee, I went into the living room. "Why don't you get dressed, and I'll make a list of places that deliver here?" We were on the edge of Kingsville, and half of the decent takeout places wouldn't come this far.

Hawk followed me, flopping on the far end of the couch and somehow managing to take up two thirds of it by spreading his top leg toward me. It gave me a good look at a tattoo of what might be stone Viking style sculptures, but I wasn't about to ask him to nudge the towel up so I could be sure.

"Your choice," he said. "I've got cash for whatever you want."

As I scrolled through the list, it was impossible not to think about the wall of tanned skin beside me. "How about pizza?" I asked.

"Oh, I think we can do better than that, can't we?"

Hawk slid over until his thigh was pressed against mine as he studied my phone. He must have noticed how my breath hitched, and the phone shook slightly.

His hand reached out to cover mine, steadying my grip. "How about that place?" he said. "Do you like Indian food?"

"Of course."

His warm breath skimmed along my cleavage. He glanced down, then chuckled. "I didn't know anyone liked Indian food that much," he said, raising an eyebrow and staring pointedly at my chest.

Looking down, I saw my nipples had hardened into sharp points. "Stop it," I snapped, more embarrassed than angry.

Hawk slowly backed away, nodding with a seductive smile. "Order us three butter chickens, chicken tikka masala, some samosas, a whole bunch of naan, and anything else you want. Thanks."

He stood up and walked away, the towel stretched

perfectly over his sculpted ass. "I'd better put some clothes on before I distract you any more."

My shaking thumbs flew across the screen, selecting the food he wanted.

I'd moved here because it was the cheapest place I could find that still seemed relatively safe while I discovered my new solo identity. My goal was peace and quiet without my family controlling my every move.

One of the many things on my list of things to discover with my newfound freedom was what sort of man I would be interested in. I'd never been permitted to even consider dating a boy without my father's background check and my mother's seal of approval after checking his social status.

But Hawk wasn't a boy, he was a man. Older, wild, and untamed. He was real. He was definitely the sort of man I was looking for. And geez – I'd already seen all of him.

Was he actually interested, or just the sort of cocky guy who flirted with every woman who was conveniently there?

Now that we were living together, I was going to be conveniently there at all times.

2

———————

HAWK

So much for swearing off relationships forever.

There was no doubt in my mind that Lila was my dream girl. I'd sketched women's faces quite a bit back in art school, and later when I became a tattoo artist, and my default ideal female face was very similar to Lila's.

Brooke had warned me that Ashley was fairly quiet and Lila was quite shy. She had made me promise not to be annoying.

In my eyes, this was Lila's space, and I wanted to keep it that way and find a way to fit into her world. But that meant I would have to get to know her very quickly.

From the way she stared at my body, I knew she was at least interested physically. I'd use that to full advantage. That is, if I could stop dreaming about her midnight blue eyes long enough to think straight.

I threw on a pair of dark blue sweatpants and a black tank top so that I matched her Friday night loungewear vibe. I went back to the living room with a blanket in my hand. "Your space is already decorated, and I like it. But I've kept this blanket on the couch every place I've ever lived. Do you mind?"

I tossed it along the back of the couch between us as I sat down. "It's lovely," Lila said, running her fingers along the yarn. "Why not?"

"Apparently my great aunt crocheted it," I said with a shrug. "I just think it's a really nice blue."

"This is your space, too. Feel free to add your own touches," she said sweetly.

The only thing I wanted to touch was her hand as it dragged along the blanket. Somehow I was going to have to find a way to control myself until I knew how she felt.

Her phone rang with the food delivery, so I grabbed my wallet and ran to meet the guy halfway down the stairs.

I could see why this place was so cheap. It was a small, old warehouse divided up into several apartments. Although there was plenty of space, there was no elevator, and it was bound to be freezing come winter.

By the time I got back, Lila was arranging plates and cutlery on the coffee table in the living room area. "Did you want to watch a movie while we eat?" she asked.

I tried to think of the best way to get her talking freely. "I can't focus on a movie when there's this much amazing food," I said, placing containers on the table. "But they just put some remake of old quiz shows online. Do you want to play?"

"Sure." There was something in her tone that made me curious.

Halfway through the show, I figured out why. Lila was fiercely competitive, with a depth and breadth of knowledge that impressed the hell out of me.

Pausing the show, I turned to her. "Okay, genius. I'm fine getting my ass handed to me by a little pipsqueak of a girl, I just need to know how. Are you one of those child prodigy brainiacs or something?"

Her laugh was delightful. "I was one of those kids who had a book permanently blocking my face. Then I went to university early, and did two years of general arts. It covers a wide variety of topics, I guess."

I couldn't stop my eyes from wandering along her luscious cleavage. "I bet the university guys went wild for you," I muttered.

A soft blush crept across those perfect cheekbones. "It was an all-girls' school," she whispered.

"Damn. They still have those?"

She nodded, those big eyes suddenly drenched in sorrow. "If you have super strict parents, that's your only option." Her frown made my heart ache for her.

"I know a bit about overprotective, pushy parents." Taking her hand, I kissed the back of it gently. "There's a man of the house here to protect you now, Lila. I've got your back, okay?"

She smirked. "You've been here less than eight hours. You can't just declare yourself the man of the house."

"Oh yeah? How old are you?"

That blush was so damn sexy. "Twenty."

"Well, I'm thirty-seven. So, therefore, I'm in charge."

She pulled her hand back and lightly smacked my arm. "You're not the boss of me, mister." Her eye roll and hair toss were adorably childish, but the look in those breathtaking eyes was extremely adult. I loved that she couldn't stop checking me out.

Strict parents and an all-girls' school? This sweet little angel might not have had much of an opportunity to date or be with men at all.

That thought sent my blood south, and when my cock

shifted in my sweatpants it certainly caught Lila's eye. "Don't worry," I teased. "He's just upset that you didn't shake hands when you met him earlier."

Her giggle shook those perky tits.

"It's not too late," I said, stretching my arm out behind her on the couch. "A polite introduction is one of the foundations of a civilized society."

Lila raised her hand, and for a split second, I honestly thought she was going to grab my dick. It twitched again as if trying to reach up to meet her. Then she leaned past me to grab the remote and turn the show back on, making me laugh out loud harder than I had in quite some time.

Lila was saucy, smart, and had an energy that was already driving me crazy.

So much for my plan to take a year off to find myself.

I'd found Lila. We belonged together. That was clear already.

3

———

LILA

Saturday mornings used to be torture. Brunch, manicure, hair stylist, shopping, and preparing for whatever ridiculous social event Mom had me booked for that evening.

Apparently a *young lady of my status* was supposed to be seen at events so that she would *stay top of mind* when suitors were looking for brides, and when the glitterati were deciding who to invite to the next round of parties. I was also forced to spend time with a group of girls my own age that my parents decided were suitable friends.

I hated it.

Rolling out of bed at nine and indulging in twenty minutes of yoga today was sheer bliss. I had nothing on the agenda other than clean the apartment, read, and enjoy my freedom.

Now that the basics were taken care of – food, shelter, job – nothing else really mattered. Well, almost nothing. As I folded into downward dog, I thought of my incredibly sexy, strangely forthright new roommate.

He was wildly outgoing, in a way that felt right for me.

In the past, I'd been dragged out of my comfort zone by my parents every single day. This was more like a gentle push. It felt a lot healthier.

Normally I would have lounged around the apartment in my pajamas, but I wanted Hawk to see me at my best for at least our first weekend together. That is, if he even spent time here. For all I knew, I might hardly ever see him.

Pulling on black leggings and a simple blue dress that was flattering but also incredibly comfortable, I put the front of my tousled hair up in a clip and opened my bedroom door.

I smelled coffee, and something sweet cooking. When I reached the kitchen I stopped in my tracks. Hawk was standing in front of the stove wearing nothing but brown board shorts.

From the back, he looked like a surfer, muscular and tan. It was wild what the sight of his body did to me. Flutters were zipping through my stomach, over my breasts, between my thighs. My mouth became dry, and my breathing became shallow.

Total, overwhelming, intoxicating lust. I'd never experienced the sensation before. It was much stronger than I imagined.

"Hey there, sleepyhead," Hawk said, spinning to flash me a wide grin that revealed perfect teeth. He came over to take me by the shoulders and direct me to a kitchen chair. "Park that sweet little ass right here."

In seconds I had coffee and banana chocolate pancakes in front of me.

"I figured the new man of the house should prove his worth," he said with a chuckle. "Don't worry – I'll get the next round of groceries."

"Wow, thank you."

He sat down beside me instead of across from me. Was that so that his thigh could brush mine as we ate?

Everything about him was so direct. He didn't play games. There was no map of appropriate talking points like my mother always made me memorize before any social event. Hawk just spoke whatever was on his mind with no filter. I admired that.

"These are delicious," I said, trying to slow down so that I didn't gobble my breakfast in front of him.

"Thanks. I'm not the greatest cook, but these usually turn out pretty well." His phone beeped, and he looked at it with a frown.

"Something wrong?"

He shrugged. "Just short staffed at work today. But we'll get through." Hawk turned and flashed that incredible grin again. "So what do you do for a living? Model? Game show hostess? No...weather girl. That must be it."

My hand hovered in front of my mouth to hide the possible pancake crumbs in my teeth while I laughed. After a second, I managed to say, "I'm the receptionist at a small physiotherapy office. They specialize in patients who've just had hip and knee replacements."

Those striking brown eyes grew wide, then he grabbed the phone and called someone. "Hey, Lars – crisis averted. I've got a receptionist for the day. We'll be there at ten."

As soon as he ended the call, I sputtered, "What are you talking about?"

"Hey, you can't leave your new roommate high and dry, right? Did you have any important plans today that you can't cancel?"

I shook my head. "No."

He looked me up and down again. "You're already dressed perfectly. Trust me on this one."

I honestly did.

Twenty minutes later, Hawk's arm was tightly around me as we walked into Briar Street Tattoo Shop.

Their usual receptionist Heather had the flu, but luckily she was incredibly organized. In minutes I had everything under control – answering the phone, letting each artist know when their next appointment was arriving, and welcoming people to the shop.

It was an extremely different clientele than my usual job, but most of the tasks were the same on my end.

All five of the tattoo artists were booked solid for the day, but they all took a few moments to chat to me, and anyone waiting in the lobby, as they arrived.

Hawk made a point of putting his arm around me any time they came close. I guess he wanted to give the impression that we were together. But why? Was he afraid that one of his friends would hit on me? Would that bother him?

It certainly bothered me when his one o'clock appointment was someone named Alex, but thank goodness it turned out to be a guy. I honestly didn't know if I could handle watching Hawk's hands all over another woman's skin.

As the day went on, his arm around my shoulder slipped to my waist. His innocent snuggles pulled us closer together. Hawk couldn't keep his hands off me, and didn't care who saw it.

I loved it. It made me feel like his. Yet it felt like things were going in the wrong order. He hadn't even asked me out. We hadn't even kissed.

Kissing him was the only thing I could think about every time he spoke. Those lips. His faintly smoky, earthy scent. Those huge hands that gripped me whenever he guided me around the shop.

Before I knew it, the shop was closing and Hawk latched his arm around me as we went back to his truck.

"You were a trooper today, Lila," he said, backing me up against the passenger side door. "Thank you."

"I was glad to help. Plus, the extra money doesn't hurt."

He smirked. "I don't think you did it for the money. I think you wanted to help your man out of a desperate situation. Didn't you?"

My head fell back as I laughed, and he leaned in, placing a single kiss at the hollow of my throat. My breath caught, then his hands gripped my hips. As his mouth approached mine, I had to hold back a whimper. I'd never wanted anything so much in my life.

A car drove by, the rev of the engine completely spoiling the mood. "Let me get you home and feed you," Hawk said, helping me into the truck. "Can't let the girl who saved the day go hungry."

As we drove home, his hand reached out to tap my knee now and then. He was so casual about touching me. Why wouldn't he kiss me properly?

Maybe he was simply teasing me because I was a woman in his space, and he thought it was amusing. Maybe he thought I was too shy to be interested in someone like him.

The time for teasing was over. I wanted a kiss from those perfect lips, and I had to find a way to make that happen immediately.

4

HAWK

As I drove us home, stopping briefly for takeout, my mind was churning. I needed to kiss Lila. Why was I hesitating? I was sure she wanted me to.

Maybe it was that she was so innocent. Something in her eyes told me that she wasn't used to being with men. If indeed it was her first kiss, I had to make it memorable.

I also couldn't make her feel cornered. Having a guy suddenly living in her space was enough to deal with, and I knew that my energy was a bit over the top sometimes.

I had probably overstepped my bounds when we were at the shop. But I couldn't let the other guys think for one second that Lila might be available. I had to find out what she was thinking.

We got home and had dinner, with Lila kicking my ass again at some of those weird trivia shows. When it started to get late, I caught Lila yawning.

"Rough day at the office?" I chuckled.

She rolled her eyes at me. "I did have a busy day of lounging planned, you know."

"I'm sorry. Did you want the new man of the house to

tuck you into bed?"

She tried to glare, but ended up giggling. "Stop teasing me," she said, tapping her foot into my leg. "Stop acting like —" Those beautiful lips snapped shut.

This was my moment. Scooping Lila up in my arms, I walked toward her bedroom. She didn't protest, snuggling into my chest as if she were delighted to be there.

Setting her down, I said, "I'm closing the door for sixty seconds to let you change into your pajamas, then I'm coming in."

I heard scurrying before I even had the door shut. Around a minute later, I cracked the door an inch open.

"All clear," she called out.

Lila was already under the covers. I sat on the edge of her bed, fluffing her pillows and shaking her enough to make her grin.

"Am I the first man who's been in your bedroom?" I asked gently.

"Yes."

Leaning down, my thumb trailed along her jaw as I stared into those beautiful indigo eyes. "Has any man ever kissed you...while you were in bed?"

She smiled saucily, and her head shook slowly against my hand. For a split second I wondered whether I should ask for permission, but then she leaned up, meeting me halfway as our lips connected.

Instantly my senses were overloaded with her sweet fragrance, the softness of her skin, and her indescribable warmth. Our mouths moved together perfectly as the kiss deepened and my arms slipped around her.

I would have expected Lila's kiss to be tentative. Instead, her hands wound into the back of my hair, pulling me closer to lie down next to her in the bed.

Her hot little body under mine made my pulse quicken, the rush of lust swirling in my rigid cock as my breath caught in my chest.

I'd always been confident with women. Now, I was second-guessing every move. I needed this moment to be perfect. To let Lila know that I cared for her, not just the wildly luscious body that was squirming under me.

Her soft moan as my tongue slipped into her mouth made my fingers tighten against her skin. Lila rubbed her breasts against my chest, gasping as I cradled her body under mine. It felt like she wanted all of me, right now. I could have torn our clothing off and taken her immediately.

But as my lips lingered on hers, I forced myself to slow down. I couldn't ruin this by rushing. Since I was older, I really was going to have to pretend I was wiser, and do the right thing.

"Sweet dreams, gorgeous," I whispered, giving her one more searing hot kiss before laying her back on the pillow.

"Good night, Hawk." That sweet voice was going to bounce around my heart all night long.

I left her room and closed the door, then went into my new space and flopped down on the bed.

My name sounded so sweet on her lips. Maybe that was because she didn't know my other name.

I was the only one of my relatives ever to think that the family name was something to be hidden. But I wanted to be known on my own merit.

Some day, when Lila knew me better, I'd tell her how I had left my family circle. Hopefully she would laugh. And hopefully she would realize that it didn't have anything to do with who I was now.

All I had ever wanted to be with my own person. And now, Lila's man.

5

LILA

I got up quietly, tiptoeing around as I put the coffee on. As much as I adored Hawk's company, I did want some time alone. My long Sunday morning bath was a ritual I loved.

Back at my parents' home, one of the maids would draw a bath and fuss around with various fragrances, trying to anticipate what I wanted, not realizing that what I truly desired was to do things for myself.

As I filled the tub, I drizzled in a bit of vanilla shampoo, which basically did the job of a bubble bath. Money was super tight since I had only been able to make one withdrawal against my father's credit card before leaving. I was too afraid to use it again, for fear he might track me.

Lighting a couple of cheap supermarket candles, I slipped lazily into the bath with my coffee mug beside me.

Heaven. Peace. Tranquility.

Except that my mind was whirling every time I thought of Hawk.

Last night's kiss had shaken me to the core. I'd always

assumed that I would date someone for quite a while before I would consider getting physical.

With Hawk, everything was instant. I didn't think, I felt.

I heard footsteps around the apartment, and a few clinks as he poured himself a coffee. Then silence again. Knowing he was out there while I was luxuriating naked under the bubbles made me giggle.

There was a tap at the door. "Hey, Lila, are you going to be very long?"

"I'm in the bath."

There was a low chuckle. "Just give me a second to imagine that."

I could picture his handsome grin on the other side of the door.

"I was thinking of getting an extra bookshelf for the living room," he said. "I just found one online that would look perfect, but it comes in two colors and the sale is only on for today. Can I reach my phone in and show you?"

From the angle of the tub, he wouldn't have to open the door very far to be able to see me completely. But since I'd already gotten a good look at him, I couldn't help feeling that he would think that fair was fair.

"I swear I won't peek," he added.

He might have been lying. Yet I didn't care. I wanted him to see me. I wanted him to feel total desire when he looked at me.

Hawk obviously thought that I was a shy little girl. What if, just for today...I wasn't? What if I tried on the persona of an outgoing woman, to see what it felt like?

Standing up, I hoped that he didn't hear my voice shaking as I said, "Come on in."

The door opened and a phone floated in as he reached it toward me. "White wood or dark?"

I was shocked that he didn't actually peek in. It made me want him even more. "I'm not sure. You'd better come in so I can get a proper look."

"Okay..." he said slowly, sticking his head around the edge of the door.

His mouth fell open, then he froze. Having his eyes drinking in my wet, naked figure made my heart speed up while my stomach tightened. My nipples hardened into points, and not just because I was slightly chilly. Then Hawk's eyes met mine, and I ran my tongue along my lower lip.

His phone clattered to the floor as he lunged for me, grabbing a towel and scooping me up in his arms. In a flash I was carried out and laid across his bed, as his lips sucked gently at my breasts.

"Tell me to stop and I'll put you right back in the tub," he growled. "Otherwise, I need to eat this luscious pussy right now."

How was a girl supposed to respond to that?

Lacking words, I simply let my thighs fall open as his hand slid down my stomach. My fingers tangled in his thick hair as he kissed my breasts, slowly switching from one to the other before nibbling a trail lower.

His strong hands spread my thighs wide as he settled between them, staring at my damp, naked flesh. He looked up to meet my eyes, and I gave him a single nod.

Then I gasped as his tongue dove straight through my center. Although it felt like Hawk was genuinely starving for me, his movements were slow and gentle. Every single touch made me feel cared for. Adored.

My feelings for this strangely confident man were growing by the second as his palms caressed my inner thighs. How could I be so comfortable with him while also feeling like he was sending electrical surges all through my body?

His tongue explored every fold and curve of my skin, then he circled my swollen nub before sweeping straight across it. My hips shifted and my fingers trailed around the outside of his ears, caressing any bit of skin I could reach.

"Easy, gorgeous," he murmured. His warm breath drifted across me, sending more shivers up my spine. "Just be still and come on my tongue."

Nobody had ever said anything like that to me before. Lying back, I tried to relax as his tongue slipped slowly over and around my sensitive clit. His fingers began exploring my entrance, circling several times before tentatively gliding inside. I could feel how wet I was as he moved inside me.

"You're so sexy," Hawk's deep voice rasped. "Give it to me, baby. Let me feel you."

Tension was already building as every single muscle seemed to prickle in anticipation. Knowing that this incredible man genuinely thought I was sexy shifted something in my mind.

I didn't need to be proper anymore. I only had to feel and experience life for myself.

"Yes," I whispered. "Mmm, just a little more..."

His tongue began lapping steadily quicker as I felt myself falling. My thighs clamped around his head as I screamed – a flash of energy surging through me as I came so hard I couldn't see for a moment.

As I stared into Hawk's eyes, I could feel his satisfaction was as deep as my own. He wanted me.

I wasn't just some girl who happened to be in his cousin's apartment. Hawk was feeling the same deep, gut-wrenching pull that I was.

But even though I dearly wanted it to happen, I wasn't yet sure whether I could let us be real, with all of the baggage that would come with that.

6

HAWK

I'd never felt peace like this. After all of the arguing with my relatives to be who I wanted to be, everything with Lila was simple.

Tasting her sweet, fresh pussy had been the highlight of my existence up till now, but it was her soft cries and the way her fingers curled gently around my ears that made me realize.

She was the one.

Lifting her in my arms, I wrapped her in the towel and brought her back into the bathroom. Running some hot water to warm up the tub, I held her hand and helped her slip back in.

Looking around on the floor, I found my phone, then held it out to her. "Which shelf?"

"To go in front of the big south window?"

"Yeah – I was thinking we could spread out the stuff from the other shelves so it wasn't as crowded, maybe add some plants."

"I'm fine with either, but I think the darker wood might look nicer."

"Done. I'll be back later with dinner." I kissed her forehead, then left the apartment with a spring in my step.

Good God, I'd gone domestic.

This was not what this year was supposed to be about. I was supposed to be running wild and finding myself and doing whatever else men did when they were on the verge of a midlife crisis and trying to extricate themselves from family obligations.

I should have been buying a bright red sports car right about now.

Too late. Lila had me hooked. I wanted nothing more than to have dinner with her on the couch and find out about her life, getting her to open up to me.

Several hours later, we were doing exactly that, except Lila wouldn't really share anything about her past.

"Tell me about that all-girls university," I said. "Is your family super religious or something?"

She shook her head. "No. It's just where my mother went."

She popped another piece of broccoli into her mouth so that I couldn't ask further questions for a few moments. After asking several more questions about where she was from, and her family, I realized there was no subtle way to ask her to lower the wall she had around that part of her life.

"Hey," I said gently, placing my hand on her knee. "I can tell you're running from something. I just hope that you're running toward something good."

Those incredible deep blue eyes stared at me, then she whispered, "Me too."

"I'll help you any way I can, Lila. But I can't slay a dragon if I can't see it. Do you know what I mean?"

I held out my arms, and she snuggled into them. "Yes. I'm just not ready to go there yet. Is that okay?"

Stroking her hair, I murmured, "Absolutely. You take all the time you want. Just know that I want to keep you safe and happy."

My lips dropped to her hair. "And of course, I'm wildly curious. Until you say otherwise, I'm going to assume that you are the princess of some country I've never heard of, and you're not ready to accept the crown or something."

She spun, raising an eyebrow. Apparently I'd struck a nerve.

"Of course, you could also just be hiding here to keep your new boyfriend away from everyone," I said, trying to sound serious. "Just one look at me, and you're terrified that your seven sisters and forty-two cousins might come running to steal me away."

Lila's giggle was pure delight.

I grabbed the blanket from the back of the couch, wrapping it around her as we curled up to watch a movie. It was the perfect Sunday night. Now if only I could get Lila to unload the rest of her secrets so that we could start this relationship properly, I would be the happiest man on earth.

I just hoped that they were secrets I was prepared to deal with, since I hadn't told her mine yet.

7

LILA

I woke up ten minutes early even without my alarm, with no idea how I got into bed. I must have fallen asleep on the couch with Hawk. It was touching how careful he was with me.

The apartment was quiet. A note in the kitchen read, "Have a great day, little woman. Text me when you need a ride home."

Little woman? Argh. Hawk was amazing, but that 'man of the house' stuff could stop anytime.

Somehow I made it through the workday with the fluttering feeling in my core staying relatively in check.

I always wondered what it would feel like to have a man in my life. A real man that I chose for myself. Well, I guess I didn't really choose Hawk. He just sort of appeared in a flash. Flesh. In the flesh.

A lot of flesh.

I couldn't stop that image of him naked from popping into my mind at the worst possible times. I definitely needed to see that view again as soon as possible.

Me: I'm leaving the office at 5:30, but I'm fine getting home by myself.

Hawk: Where is your office? Address, please. You will be picked up.

It was strange that I absolutely adored his overprotective nature. In my old life, people acted like I couldn't do anything for myself and it drove me bonkers. Now I was fully capable of doing whatever I wanted, but letting Hawk in just felt good.

At some point I was going to have to tell him who I was, and what was expected of me. It was probably rude to let it go on too long before mentioning that I was basically in hiding.

But it might change Hawk's opinion of me. I wanted him to see the new me, the one who was not under her mother's thumb, and controlled by her weird high society standards.

Around five, Hawk sent a text.

Hawk: Look for my truck out front at 5:30.

I went about my end of the day duties, sending out appointment reminder emails and tidying up. When I left the office, there was a huge tattooed man leaning in front of Hawk's truck. As I got closer, I recognized the owner of the tattoo shop.

"Lars, right?" I asked.

"Yeah." He politely took my elbow to help hoist me into the truck, then we drove toward the shop. "Hawk is just finishing up a job that took a bit longer than he anticipated. He didn't want you waiting around, or taking the bus."

"I'm so sorry. I don't mean to be any trouble."

Lars laughed. "Hell no, don't even think like that."

As we paused at a red light, he held up his phone. His lock screen photo was a pretty woman holding a baby. "I'm the only married guy in the shop, which means apparently

I'm safe and responsible enough to drive you," he chuckled. "He also insisted I take his truck instead of my motorbike."

"Wow." I paused, wondering how nosy I could be. "So, have you known Hawk for a long time?"

"Oh, yeah. He's cruised out this way every few years. At first it was sporadic, and we just gave him a few shifts doing walk-ins. He's always been a great artist, but he moved around a lot. He's here full-time now, because...well, I'm sure you know."

"No, why?"

"Oh." Lars gave me a sideways glance. "Well, that's not exactly my story to tell. You're going to have to ask him."

Well, crap. I'd been hoping for a shortcut to get to know Hawk better.

"He really is a great guy," Lars said, shooting me a grin. "And he's absolutely crazy about you."

I had no idea what to say to that. The thought of someone as incredible as Hawk liking me that much was hard to believe.

We got to the shop just as Hawk was finishing up a tattoo around a man's forearm.

"Hey, baby," he called out, making sure that everyone could hear. It felt like he was publicly claiming me, which I had to admit, made me feel amazing. "I'll just be another few minutes, then I'll pick up groceries and make you dinner."

I'm not sure why that made my rebellious streak kick in. While he was busy with his client, I told Lars, "I'm just going to the sandwich shop next door. Don't let him freak out."

Even though I didn't have much money, Hawk shouldn't be buying dinner every single night.

I couldn't explain to him that after having been coddled my entire life, being independent was part of the new identity I was trying to form. I was sure he would forgive me. Every man on the planet loved a great sandwich.

Hawk pretended to be upset that I "disobeyed the man of the house" on the way home, but honestly we couldn't stop laughing about it.

He insisted on carrying the take-out bag as we walked into our building, and as we were starting up the stairs, we ran into Dana, the downstairs neighbor.

After introducing Hawk, I realized that I hadn't really had a chance to speak to anyone about my instant relationship. I'd had to desert my mother-appointed friends when I left my family, and I hadn't made many friends besides Ashley and Brooke.

"Why don't you go ahead," I suggested. "Dana and I haven't had a chance to catch up for a while. "

"No problem, baby," he said, kissing the top of my head before bounding up the stairs.

Dana turned to me with wide eyes. "*Baby*? Apparently the shy little girl upstairs has been keeping secrets."

I quickly explained how Brooke had sublet the room to her cousin.

"And all that man just...showed up in your home?" Dana laughed with an expressive wave of her hand.

We had only hung out a handful of times, and gone out for drinks twice, but I really liked Dana. She was forthright, and gave great big sister advice when I needed it.

Her laughter faded away, and her expression turned serious. "Sweetie, no offense, but when you first moved in you seemed pretty sheltered. Now you're living with a weapons grade hottie? Are you okay with flipping from zero to sixty in a microsecond?"

I sighed, leaning back against the brick wall as I nodded. "I likely would have freaked out a few months ago. But now that my entire life is..." I certainly couldn't get into the details. "Let's just say, in flux...it feels like it's the right time for big changes, you know?"

Dana nodded, then looked me dead in the eye. "Is he sweet to you?"

"Definitely."

"Does he listen to you, and value your opinions?"

"Yes. And yes."

She grinned, twirling the purple tips of her shoulder length hair in her fingers. "Well then. You should definitely let loose and have as much fun as you want. Go for it. You deserve it."

"Thanks. I appreciate it." Dana always seemed to have such a positive energy that I truly valued her opinion.

She headed for the door, and I asked, "Where are you off to?"

"My friend's band is in town," she said. "They usually need somebody to work either the door or the merch table, so I'm going to show up and surprise them."

"Cool – have a great time!"

The quick chat made me feel a lot better. It was like I had a buddy's stamp of approval. It was hard not to second guess myself when I'd never been in a relationship before and had no idea what I was doing.

By the time I got upstairs, Hawk had set the sandwiches on the nicest pair of plates in our mismatched pile. He had even lit candles.

"Thanks, this is lovely."

Hawk scooped me up and set me on the couch. "It's the least I could do considering my girl didn't let me make her dinner," he grumbled, but his eyes were dancing.

"Right. I'm supposed to remember that you're the manly man of the house," I laughed.

"Damn straight."

As he sat close beside me, I realized I loved the ridiculous way he teased me. Then it hit me that there was a secret tucked inside that thought.

I loved Hawk.

Everything about him felt like it was lighting me up from the inside. I was already starting to envision this new life with him lasting a long time, which was both exhilarating and terrifying.

If he wasn't used to staying in one place for very long, I couldn't run the risk of scaring him away.

Would he still want me when he found out who I was?

8

HAWK

lthough I was touched that Lila insisted on picking up dinner, it underlined that I hadn't even taken her on a real date yet.

As we ate our dinner, I asked all sorts of questions about her day. It sounded like the office was a nice place, and it was clear Lila loved helping people.

My girl was a sweetheart. Which made me feel even worse for not being more romantic.

Once the food had disappeared, I said, "Baby, you know that you don't have to feed me and entertain me just because I'm in your space. I mean, I'm paying rent, but I know that I was just sort of dropped on you."

Her eyelashes fluttered as she looked down, then up to smile at me. "I like it."

Looking around the loft, I saw that the moon was coming up over the edge of some buildings. Taking her hand, I led her to the window. "I'll have to remember to get you some roses. But at least we have moonlight."

Lila giggled sweetly, reaching up to clasp her hands

behind my neck and swaying. Wrapping my arms around her, we began to dance in silence.

"I don't know how to be romantic, but I'm going to try," I said. "You deserve real dates."

Her teeth drifted across her bottom lip. "Actually, I prefer private places to public, usually."

Spinning her gently in a circle, I screwed up the courage to ask. "Baby, are you hiding from someone?" When her eyes tensed, I wished I could swallow the question back down. Then she shook her head.

"I'm sorry," I said quickly. "You're not ready to talk about it. That's fine. I'm so sorry I pried."

Twirling her around, I picked her up and swung her in a circle until she laughed. "We'll have romantic dates at home," I said, setting her back on her feet. "I'm already completely infatuated with you, baby. Saturday at the shop I implied that you're my girlfriend. Is that true now?"

"If you want me," Lila whispered.

My arms tightened around her. "Want you? I've been trying to control myself since the second you first looked at my—"

Her hand clapped over my mouth. I licked her palm, and she snatched her hand back, laughing.

"Bits," I said. "Am I allowed to say that word?"

It was adorable how much she blushed.

"Come on," I drawled, taking her hand and waltzing her around the space in the moonlight. "It was the first one you've seen up close and personal. Of course you want it. Of course you want me to be your first."

Although I was teasing, Lila looked up at me and nodded very seriously.

"Excellent. So, if you're officially my girlfriend now, we should probably conserve water and shower together every morning, don't you think?" She began to laugh, and I spun her around quickly until she gasped.

"Every inch of you should be spotless before you go to work. It's very important that I make sure of these things as the ma– "

Her hand clapped over my mouth again. "Don't you dare say the man of the house." Lila attempted to look stern, failing completely.

As soon as she pulled her hand back, I said, "Okay...as the cock-owner in this relationship?"

Lila's mouth dropped open and she started laughing so hard her knees buckled. Lifting her in my arms, I asked, "Where would you like to go, my gorgeous little princess?"

She pursed those perfect lips, then whispered, "Your room."

My shaft was already thickening, then it lurched in my jeans. I had assumed that she would want to take things slowly, but I had a feeling I had underestimated my hot new girlfriend's sex drive.

Even though we were just getting started, it felt like she wanted to make up for lost time. That was fine with me.

I hoped that Lila already knew that she had my heart. Now she could take any other part of me she wanted.

9

LILA

My choice had been made. I wanted Hawk. Not just because he was an incredible symbol of my new wild and free life. I'd always craved true physical desire, but for years I didn't know if it would be possible.

As he set me down beside his bed, I unbuttoned my top. Hawk grinned, nodded, then pulled off his t-shirt.

I completely blanked as I stared at that incredible body. It was a work of art and a sinful display of pure lust all at once.

Hawk helped me by slipping off my shirt, then unhooking my bra. As he unfastened my skirt and pulled it off, I realized that I didn't want him to see me as a nervous, innocent girl. If I was going to be in touch with my sexuality, I had to own it.

"I want to see you naked," I said, though my voice wavered.

That handsome grin made my belly flutter. When his jeans and shorts hit the floor, a strange squeak emanated from my throat. It was huge. Incredibly hard. And pointing straight at me. As a single bead of pre-come slid across the tip, I realized my mouth was hanging open.

"You better close those sexy lips before a naughty man like me gets ideas," he said with a low chuckle.

I sat on the edge of his low bed and leaned forward, which brought my mouth to the perfect height. He stepped closer as I reached for his cock, wrapping my hands around the base. Looking up at him, I grinned, then opened wide.

Hawk leaned forward as I slowly dragged my tongue across the thick round head. Running my hands along the length, I noticed it was a strange texture. The skin itself was velvety soft, but underneath it was stiff and almost pulsing. It was the sexiest thing I'd ever seen.

Then I saw the look in his eyes, making me dizzy with lust. Hawk was infatuated with me. I could see that clear as day. Those expressive eyes burned into mine as his hand grazed the back of my hair.

Trying to think of what I'd read in the odd smutty bit of erotica I'd stumbled across, I moved my hands up and down the shaft while taking as much of him into my mouth as I could.

His stomach and thighs tightened. "That feels so good, baby."

When I murmured in agreement, he shuddered. Could he feel the vibrations? I tried humming gently for a moment, looking up to see his eyes positively blazing. My lips were stretched too wide to grin, yet I wondered if he could see it in my eyes.

Sucking, licking, and humming, I could feel his cock swell even more as his breathing became harsh and uneven. This sensation was so intimate. It felt like we were connecting on a much deeper level.

I was already in love with Hawk. Could he tell?

There was no way to know if he felt the same for me yet, but there was definitely something there.

For the very first time, I knew that a man wanted me for me, and not for a connection to my family. That knowledge was refreshing. I worked my hands and lips faster.

"Baby," he growled, gripping the back of my hair as he thrust carefully down my throat, "Tell me quickly if you don't want to swallow. Otherwise—"

I nodded as much as I could. Having his attention completely fixated on me made me feel bonded to him. I wanted us to be as close as possible.

Moaning around his length, I sucked harder, massaging his slippery skin as I felt him throb in my mouth. Then he made a choked noise like a frantic growl, his movement slowing as his cock surged and pulses of warm liquid gushed down my throat. I managed to swallow several times, continuing my motions until he pulled his length from my lips.

Hawk's mouth hung open, then he breathed, "Lila, you're incredible."

He collapsed on the bed, pulling me with him and holding me so tight that for a few glorious seconds, I truly believed that he never wanted to let me go.

10

HAWK

I'd never felt such complete and utter satisfaction. From the second I first saw that beautiful doll-like face, I knew Lila was the one. The way she touched me with such tender sweetness told me that she felt the same.

Once my heart rate was almost back to normal after the most intense climax of my life, I kissed her gently. Then I shifted, tucking a pillow under her head as I nuzzled my way down her body.

Slipping her panties down her shapely legs, I draped her calves over my shoulders and dove right into her unbelievable pink pussy. She tasted so fresh. So dewy soft.

The way Lila's hips moved under me as I devoured her excited me even more than my own orgasm. I needed to feel her lose herself for me. As I swirled my tongue around her clit, gently pushing my middle finger inside, those intoxicating gasps and sighs filled me with pride.

I was going to be her man. Not in the way my mother always preached, to pair up for the sake of society, and to bring honor to the family. Bullshit.

I was going to be Lila's man because she wanted me. Not needed, wanted.

Removing my finger, I plunged my tongue into her depths as she moaned. Then I went back to licking her clit steadily, feeling the tension growing as her silky thighs tightened around my shoulders.

"Come for me, gorgeous," I rasped in a low growl. "Let me taste you."

"Yes," she barely breathed as her body began to quiver. "Oh my...Hawk..."

Her soft scream reverberated around the room as I felt her gush around my finger. Placing a hand on her belly to keep her still throughout her climax, I stared into those breathtaking indigo eyes.

When she stopped twitching, I kissed my way up her body to claim her lips as she clung to me.

We were both naked, and her soft little pussy was dripping wet. I could have easily plunged inside her in a heartbeat. But Lila was clearly shy. Thoughtful. She might want to take her time.

I threw a blanket over us and cuddled her into my arms. "Sleep next to me?"

Lila giggled. "You expect me to be able to sleep after something like that?"

My lips grazed her forehead. "If you want more, you're going to have to beg for it."

Her laugh was enchanting. Those magical eyes looked up at me as I caressed every inch of her that I could reach. "Sleeping or begging, baby?"

Her shy blush spoke volumes, then she slipped her hand into the back of my hair. "I think we both want the same thing."

Leaning over, I trailed my lips along her throat. "Are you so riled up you can't sleep yet?"

"Yes."

"Mmm," I murmured against her pulse point that was starting to beat more rapidly. "Is it because mine is the first cock you've seen, and now you can't get enough of it?"

Her head fell back with a laugh as she gently tugged the back of my hair. "Stop it."

"Never."

She released my hair to give me a tiny smack in the center of my chest. "Stop teasing me."

"You love it," I grinned.

Her hand moved in a slow circle, caressing my chest. Rolling her on top of me, I let my hands wander all over the perfect curve of her ass.

"Since you're such a tough chick, I'll let you be in control. Do whatever you want, baby." I continued lightly massaging her hips and behind, but made no move to go further.

Lila placed her forehead to mine and whispered, "You know what I want."

I shrugged. "I'm not a mind reader, Lila. You're going to have to either tell me, or...take matters into your own hands. So to speak."

Maybe it wasn't the most romantic time to be teasing her, but I wanted to keep things light-hearted so that she didn't become overwhelmed.

Her luscious breasts pressed firmly against my chest as she kissed me. I could feel her desire, her determination.

Then her delicate hand slipped down between us to massage my cock as it sprang back to life. Lila straddled me, spreading her legs wide as she rubbed my length suggestively.

"That's it," I breathed against her lips. "If that's what you want, baby, just take it."

A deep shudder ran through me as she ran the head of my shaft through her soaking crease.

"Wait. Do I need a condom?"

Her nose crinkled as she shook her head. "I'm on the pill."

"I knew you were smart."

She managed to fit the head between her inner lips, then I grabbed her ass hard.

"Lila, I already adore you. You don't have to prove anything to me, baby. We can wait as long as you like if you're nervous."

She shook her head. "I want you," she said softly. "Now."

When I heard her speak those words, I realized two important things.

One, I was already an inch inside her. Two, I was already completely, hopelessly, in love with my breathtaking new roommate.

11

LILA

I was more than ready. Mom had put me on the pill when I turned eighteen, just in case. The thought of a family pregnancy scandal was terrifying to her.

I wasn't opposed to the idea at the time. I wanted to take control of my own body, and be open to all possibilities.

Thank goodness, because as Hawk's body entered mine, I couldn't imagine having anything between us. I leaned up slightly to adjust the angle, placing my hands on his shoulders as I shimmied my hips from side to side.

I loved the way he stared at my breasts so hungrily. He genuinely seemed obsessed with me. The way he treated me like I was something precious filled me with a wave of confidence I'd never experienced before.

Hawk loved me for me. He didn't know where I came from, or who my family was.

Spreading my knees as wide as I could, I captured a bit more of his length. I moved up and down slowly, working his cock just a bit deeper.

"You feel so perfect, gorgeous." His low groan sent chills up my spine.

Hawk was too thick for me to take any more of him at this angle. He let me experiment for a moment, then asked, "Do you want me to take over, baby?"

Nodding, I whispered, "Yes, please."

His arms scooped around me as he carefully rolled us so that I was under him. I felt caged by his huge hard body, yet he was so warm and gentle that I felt completely safe.

"Look into my eyes, Lila," he whispered, lining himself up carefully. "Now take a slow breath."

I had just begun to inhale when he plunged deeper. The shock knocked all of the air out of me in a wash as I gasped, fingers clawing at the back of his shoulders while I shook.

"Easy," he murmured, brushing his lips against mine. "Just breathe."

The heat of that huge cock inside me, coupled with the odd sensation of being stretched and pulled open, was a lot to take. But his slow movements and the way he caressed me so sweetly took the edge off. After a moment, the most indescribable pleasure began to overtake me.

His blinking had slowed when I looked up into his eyes. "Lila," he rasped, "I've never felt anything so perfect."

My body relaxed, helping him take longer, deeper strokes. Soon he was inside me completely, my body sheathed around his.

His thumb brushed my hair from my eyes, then drifted along my cheekbone. "You're mine now," he whispered. "You're stuck with me forever."

I would have giggled, but he shifted, the base of his shaft rubbing against my clit, and a lightning bolt of pleasure raced through me with every languid stroke.

"That's it," he murmured, holding me against his chest as his hips and thighs propelled him deeper in a slow, dreamy rhythm. "Feeling you come on my cock is going to be the highlight of my life, baby."

I couldn't tell whether he was being romantic or filthy, and I didn't care. Hawk was both. It was one of the things I loved about him.

It felt like time slowed, until there was nothing in the universe beyond our bodies moving together as one. Feeling so completely full was wildly erotic. The pressure was building, as if the explosion of a lifetime was moments away.

From Hawk's shuddering breath and the tension in his shoulders as he moved over me, I could tell he was close to the edge as well. Shifting, I wrapped my legs around him, spreading wider so that there was more friction exactly where I needed it.

There was no way I could control my moans, or the way my head thrashed from side to side. I was helpless, under a spell of mind-blowing pleasure that flowed through me from head to toe.

My pussy tightened around him as my breath caught. Instead of screaming, a series of sharp gasps rattled through my lungs, and I came in waves.

"That's it," Hawk said, his voice darkening with lust as he stared down at me, thrusting faster. "You feel so good, baby. My gorgeous, perfect girl."

Was it strange that the twinge of obsession in his voice when he said I was his sent me hurtling over the edge yet again?

As his huge, throbbing cock pounded harder, faster, I saw stars flicker behind my eyelids. My body was giving his unbelievable pleasure. That idea extended my climax, rattling me to my bones.

He released a gritty growl just before I felt his wet heat burst inside me.

"Yes!" I cried, clinging to him as I writhed through another wave of pleasure. "Hawk...yes."

He raised himself on his forearms, panting for a second before kissing me hard and deep. I already thought he was an incredible kisser, but this was an entirely different energy. Possessive. I loved it.

After a moment, we separated so that we could breathe, and he rolled onto his back, pulling me into his side and throwing the blanket over us again.

"That was incredible, Lila. How do you feel?"

"Exhausted, and wonderful," I whispered, snuggling against his shoulder.

I fell asleep almost immediately, but shortly afterwards I woke up for a second, feeling Hawk's hand stroking my hair.

His voice was barely a whisper, more like just mouthing words so that I didn't wake up. "I love you, Lila. Let that sink into your mind, okay?"

I wanted to tell him that I was falling for him as well, but waves of sleep were already pulling me under again.

"I love you, Lila. We're going to get married someday... beach...take over...Kingston estate..."

I couldn't understand what he was saying, but it sounded serious, and involved plans for our future.

I was so wrapped up in bliss that I couldn't tell him that there were limitations on what I could do in public. Maybe in the morning I could try to explain, without giving everything away yet.

Allowing the deep satisfaction that I had finally been able to act on my own desires to envelop me, I fell back asleep in Hawk's arms.

12

HAWK

A deep surge of happiness washed over me as I drove Lila to work Tuesday morning. Everything felt solid. I could start to imagine what our lives would be like when we were married. There was no doubt in my mind that would be happening soon.

Her sunny smile as I dropped her off was a great sign that she felt the same way. It was difficult to only give her the tiniest kiss goodbye, but her coworkers might be watching.

I had just parked the truck beside the tattoo shop when my phone rang.

Dammit. What a way to ruin a perfect morning. "Hey, Dad. What's up?"

"I have to be brief, Michael. We'll be needing you Thursday evening. You haven't moved again, have you?"

"No, I'm still here. But I already have plans, Dad. I can't—"

"You'll cancel them." There was no mistaking the tone of his voice. This was not up for debate. "It's the Burrell and

Van der Hoff engagement party. There must be a representative of our family there."

"What about Kyle?"

Dad snorted. "He took off to Monte Carlo with that little...what's her name? Jessie?"

"Jasmine," I corrected him. "They've been together for nearly a year now."

"Right. Well, he's away, and your mother and I are in France. So it's up to you."

"Little last minute, don't you think?" I hoped that he could hear the tension in my voice. I had agreed to put in a few appearances a year but only if they were life and death. Well, according to their scale.

"It's a rushed wedding, I believe," he said, lowering his voice. "Your mother believes that it's a shotgun situation."

"I'll be sure to mention that over cocktails," I muttered, pacing in the gravel by my truck.

"You're on the list plus one," Dad said, ignoring my crack. "Your mother is in the process of finding you an acceptable date."

I stood up straighter, thrilled that for the first time, I had an answer. "Actually, I already have one."

He paused. "Michael, this event is important. Your mother almost dragged us back so we could attend."

"Don't worry," I told him. "She's gorgeous, classy, and a bit quiet. We'll make the rounds, be seen, and disappear."

"Fine." I could picture Dad's glower. "I'll need her name for the RSVP."

"Lila..." Oh my god. How could I be head over heels for a woman and not even know her last name? Holding the phone away from my ear, I called out, "Okay, I'll be right there."

"Well?" Dad asked impatiently.

"Gotta go – text me the details tonight." I disconnected the call, then paced around the truck one more time.

How strange that I still didn't know such a basic detail about my precious girl. I was so caught up in getting to know the important things, like how she took her coffee, and what her sweet laugh sounded like when I teased her.

I had to assume that Lila wasn't very well off, since she was living with two roommates in a weird drafty warehouse loft. To me, the apartment was amazing, and more importantly, I had been able to move in immediately to help Brooke out.

Thank goodness I'd kept in touch with Mom's side of the family, even if she herself hadn't.

Many people go through a midlife crisis and buy a sports car or get plastic surgery. My mother decided to do a deep dive into class snobbery. I didn't understand it, or want to have anything to do with it. But now that she was trying to climb the social ladder, she ignored anyone she considered poor or lower class, like my sweet cousin Brooke, and my darling girl.

No matter. Wherever Lila came from, I knew that I wanted her. I didn't care if her parents were rich or poor, brain surgeons or coal miners.

I knew her heart.

And that we belonged together no matter what ridiculous reaction my mother had when she found out Lila was from a family she'd never heard of.

13

LILA

Hawk had a late tattoo appointment, and I was relieved that he didn't object to me getting a ride home with one of the female therapists.

When my family was wildly overprotective, it was all about our image. Hawk was genuinely concerned about me. It was sweet, although sometimes a tiny bit much.

I unlocked the apartment door, thinking an hour alone would likely be the best thing for me. It would clear my head to curl up with a book.

A voice called out, "Hello?"

I jumped, startled, then saw Ashley coming out of her bedroom. "Hey, Lila. I'm so sorry, I forgot to text you that I was coming." She smiled, jerking a thumb toward Hawk's open door. "Brooke's cousin moved in?"

"Yes. *He* did."

"What?!"

We flopped on the couch and I brought her up to speed. Ashley had been very friendly from the moment I moved in, and was the only person here who knew about my family.

She herself was the daughter of a bank president, and

came from a somewhat similar situation. Yet even though her father was overprotective, she'd managed to get a great education, a good job, and take at least some control of her life.

"Does Hawk know that you come with a ton of designer baggage?" she asked.

"No. I haven't had a chance to tell him yet."

"False." Ashley smiled as she stared me down. "You don't *want* to tell him, because you're afraid he'll see you differently."

Busted. "Yeah, you're right."

"I think you need to be clear with him," she said softly. "Start this great new relationship off by being honest and open."

I released a long sigh. "Yeah. Thanks."

"It'll be okay," she said, standing up. "If he's really the one, he'll listen with an open mind."

I looked toward her room and saw a suitcase and duffel bag. "Are you staying for a full week?"

"No. Moving out."

"What?" I jumped to my feet.

"Don't worry, my company is paying my share of the rent for another two months. But they're not sending me out of town anymore." She rolled her eyes. "Dad put a stop to it."

Her phone beeped, and she sighed when she glanced at the screen. "I have to get going."

Grabbing her in a hug, I said, "I'm going to miss you. Stay in touch, okay?"

"You know it. I left you some herbal tea and the dishes you like. I won't need them back in Oakton."

I grabbed one of her suitcases and started helping her down the stairs just as Hawk was coming up with a bag of groceries. He offered to bring down the rest of the boxes for her, and just like that, Ashley was gone.

Hawk and I were already living together, but now we were totally alone. It felt more serious.

He went straight to work making pasta. "How was your day, honey?"

"Great, until I came home. I can't believe that Ashley moved out."

"I'm sorry you'll miss your friend. Don't worry about the rent, though. I can cover it." I had no idea how much tattoo artists made, but that was good to know.

"Can I help?" I asked.

"Sure. If you could please sit right there so I can look at your pretty face from time to time, that will inspire my incredible cooking."

I slipped onto a stool across the counter, and allowed myself to stare at his perfect ass as he moved around the kitchen.

"Oh, hey," Hawk said as he chopped peppers, "Are you free Thursday night?"

"Yes."

"Great. What's your last name? It's for the RSVP."

Before I could say anything, he reached for the kitchen timer, which was on a pile of mail. "Oh. Lila Astor," he murmured, reading the top envelope. "Perfect."

My entire body froze. "What? Why is that perfect?"

He pulled out his phone and sent a quick text.

"Wait," I said, jumping to my feet.

"What?" he asked, setting down the phone and wrapping his arms around me. "It's just an engagement party. My brother and parents are all out of the country so I have to go."

Looking down at his screen, I saw the message had been

sent. My blood ran cold and I felt tears filling my eyes. "Who did you just send my name to?" I managed to whisper.

"My mother."

Hawk stepped back and stared at my face in utter confusion as tears began to spill down my cheeks. "Baby, what's wrong? It's just a dumb party that she is RSVPing to, and I'm representing the family and all that crap."

His thumb ran along my cheek to wipe away a tear. "I promise she won't put you on any telemarketing lists, if that's what you're afraid of."

I appreciated his attempt at a joke, but I felt like the rug had just been pulled out from under me.

Even worse, I had definitely heard his own last name in Mom's society circles. If it was an engagement party with family in attendance, there were going to be people she knew there.

I began to tremble as his arms tightened around me.

"Seriously, baby, please tell me what it is. If it's a money thing, I'll buy you a dress, shoes, whatever else you need. Or you don't have to go. I can go alone. I'll put in an appearance, then come home to you and we'll watch a movie."

Hawk pulled out the stool and sat me down so he could reach over to turn the heat off on the stove.

"Do your parents know where you live?" I asked miserably.

"Yes. Well, they know the city. I don't know if they have this exact address."

"The city is all it will take," I said. "Those sorts of people pretend to know each other, always looking for any excuse to make connections. Your mother will call my mother, and tell her where I am."

Looking up, I watched as Hawk's eyes grew huge. "Oh my

God." His shoulders dropped. "Have you been hiding from them? Why?"

As I tried to collect my thoughts, his jaw tightened. "If they've ever hurt you, tell me now."

Even though I was positively furious at him, that touched my heart.

"Different kind of hurt," I whispered, trying not to sniffle. "Controlling my entire life. Only letting me socialize with people they deemed suitable. Debating who I should marry in a year and a half."

Hawk reached for me, but I stopped him. "Please don't give anyone this address. Or my phone number. It's just a matter of time before they send one of my brothers after me to drag me home."

"Over my dead body," he growled. "Lila, I'm so sorry. Can I—"

I held up my hand. "Please, I just need to be alone."

I disappeared into my room and shut the door, then lay on my bed and listened to him finish dinner.

Staring at the ceiling, my mind raced back and forth. Was it my fault, because I didn't speak up fast enough? Yes. Sure, he should have minded his own business, but then again I didn't tell him the truth about my situation. I should have.

I curled up into a tiny ball under the covers, my sinking sense of dread screaming that it was all my fault. I was furious with myself.

Not only had my new life been ruined, but I was going to have to move away and leave the gorgeous man that I had just fallen for.

14

———

HAWK

I had a brother, but no sisters. And I didn't have a lot of close female friends. But I did know that when a woman said she wanted to be alone, you listened to her.

I finished making dinner and placed a large portion in a covered bowl in the fridge. Then I went to my room to eat, and sent Lila a text.

Me: I will be in my room for the rest of the night, if you want to watch a movie or whatever in the living room. Your dinner is in the fridge. Please eat something. I will drive you to work in the morning, and we don't have to talk if you don't want to yet.

After a few minutes, I got a response.

Lila: Thank you.

I was halfway through my pasta when I heard her door open and a bit of shuffling in the kitchen. Then her door shut again. I hated the feeling that she had to hide from me in her own home.

When I was done eating, I opened my laptop to look up Lila Astor. I vaguely knew of their family, but because I ignored that whole society thing, I'd never really given a damn before.

Then I found a webpage that mentioned Lila was the daughter of Fergus and Genevieve Astor.

Genevieve Astor? That was her mother?

Good lord. Even I had heard of that woman. She was a loon.

A search brought me to her blog, which was basically a combination of society gossip and ludicrous how-to articles for women who wanted to be "desirable brides".

No wonder Lila had run away.

Genevieve would definitely want her daughter to follow her advice to confirm that it worked. If Lila married any regular guy, it would prove that she and her husband did not control the family properly.

What a disgusting combination of ego, money, and caring far too much what strangers thought.

My poor sweet baby. That was too much family pressure. She would never be allowed to be seen in public with me if I weren't from that world too.

How ironic that I actually was.

I hadn't really told her about my background yet. Our relationship had started off with too many secrets. Now I was going to have to figure out how to make things right, and how to make sure that we could be together on our own terms.

But first, I was going to have to care for Lila.

In the morning I made breakfast and prepared coffee. When she came out of her room, I simply said, "Good morning," then went back to my room until she called through the door that she was ready to leave.

During the drive to work, we chatted about the weather for a bit, but that was it. As I pulled up in front of the physiotherapist office, I said, "If anyone is searching for you, you know they'll never look twice at a big old truck like this, right?"

Finally she gave me a half-hearted attempt at a smile. "That's a good point."

"Pick you up at five-thirty?"

She nodded. "Thank you."

At eleven-forty-five I had a sandwich and fresh juice delivered to her office so that she didn't have to leave the building. When I picked her up, she gave me a slightly warmer smile. "Thank you for lunch. It was wonderful not to have to go out."

"You're welcome, baby. This is just a temporary thing. You're not going to have to hide for long."

Lila shook her head sadly. "I saw a neon green sports car go by today that looked just like Gerald's."

"Your older brother?"

Her head spun as she looked at me, then her shoulders sagged. "Yes. I guess you looked me up?"

"Yeah. I saw that your mother must be...what's the polite way to say it? A handful?"

It was great to hear her laugh, even for a few seconds, but then her expression became stony again. "So you can see why I can't let them find me," she said. "I'm not going to be a pawn in my mother's weird manipulative games. I don't think that's how society is supposed to work, and her insular group of friends doesn't interest me in the slightest."

"I understand. My family are extra opinionated and constantly digging into my business. But that's only a shred of what it seems like you must have gone through."

I pulled into the parking lot behind our building.

"I'm so sorry it was so bad for you, baby."

Lila shook her head, sending her hair cascading around

her face. "Just before I left, there was a screaming match. Mom said that I had to get in line, or else." She hesitated, biting her lip. "That was three months ago. I haven't spoken to any of them since."

"We can find a way to fix this," I said.

"I don't see how." Those big, beautiful eyes were full of tears.

I went around to help her out of the truck, but she would only take my hand for a split second before dashing into the apartment and her bedroom.

Once again, I made dinner and left her some, then hid out in my own room, brainstorming how to make things right.

When a text came in, I grabbed my phone eagerly, but it was just Dad sending me the full details of tomorrow night's party.

A plan began to form. After what my poor angel had been through, I could understand that she might never want to be among those people again. But it might be the best thing for us.

I just had to convince her to put us first, and trust me completely.

15

LILA

The ride to work Thursday morning was awkward and miserable. Maybe Hawk and I got too close too soon. Now it felt like a wedge had been driven between us.

I was grateful that he was giving me some space, because if he was too sweet to me I would have cried so hard I couldn't breathe.

I wanted to reach for him. Needed him to comfort me. But I felt torn. He had real feelings for me, but if we could never be a real couple, I had to end it immediately, for his sake as much as mine.

When we got to my office, Hawk helped me down from the truck, then suddenly wrapped his arms around me, drawing me close into his chest.

"Relax," he said. There was an odd urgency to his voice as he held me silently. Taking a few deep breaths, I tried to let his strength wash over me. After a few moments, he released me.

"It's gone now, but you said something about a bright green sports car, right?"

Dammit. Why did my office have to be on such a busy street?

"I'm sending you lunch again, and I'll pick you up at five-thirty," he said. "Don't worry. I have a plan. This is all going to be fixed tonight."

I wanted to believe him. But it seemed impossible.

All day at work I used every break to look up rental prices in other cities. I wasn't going to be able to travel very far on what little money I had. Even as I was planning to run away again, my heart felt like it was being crushed by the weight of this decision.

I loved Hawk. I knew that through and through. I couldn't take a chance of being pulled back into my mother's clutches.

Hawk wanted to do the right thing and protect me, but he couldn't be with me at all times. There was no doubt in my mind that if my brother found me, he would grab me and throw me in his car. The trunk, if necessary. He would do anything to keep my parents happy and get the huge inheritance he was promised.

If I managed to stay hidden for a few more years, maybe I could meet up with Hawk again someday, and we could disappear together.

Just before five-thirty, I heard a motorcycle pull up in front of the office. Hawk came in and handed me a helmet. "Nobody will recognize you with this on. And no Astor would be caught dead on a motorbike, right?"

Laughing, he helped me strap on the helmet, then we went out to the bike. It felt so good to wrap my arms tightly around him as he carefully drove us home.

We were about halfway there when he stopped at a red light, then a flash of green appeared in my peripheral vision.

Sliding my eyes sideways, I managed to catch a glimpse of Gerald behind the wheel.

Hawk's huge hand landed on my knee, then stroked my outer thigh. It was definitely meant to calm me, but to outside eyes, it looked like a possessive biker guy fondling his woman.

Gerald barely glanced at us, peeling away when the light turned green as if he were racing.

Hawk continued driving slowly for a block, then turned away from our usual route, taking a winding way back to our apartment. As soon as we got upstairs, he took my hand and led me to the couch.

"Please thank Lars for the motorbike," I said.

"No problem. He's going to use the truck tonight to do a big grocery run. Win win."

A knock at the door made me nearly jump out of my skin.

"Delivery," Hawk said, patting my knee as he went to the door. He returned with a large flat box, and a bag.

"Normally I would never sneak into your room," he said. "But I did while you were in the shower this morning, to get your dress and shoe sizes."

I was barely irritated, just curious. "What for?" I asked.

"You're coming with me tonight to that engagement party," he said.

A shudder ran down my spine. "Hawk, I can't go anywhere public. Especially not right now."

"Baby, I have a plan. You're going to have to trust me."

"I want to. I really do. But I can't take that chance.'

My bottom lip began to tremble uncontrollably. "Hawk," I whispered, "My mother. She's just so..." He waited patiently, patting my knee. "*Vicious*. I had to be so perfect around her. My hair, my nails, the arch of my eyebrows. I couldn't eat pizza before she needed me to attend a function because I might bloat."

Hawk's eyes grew huge as he waited for me to continue.

"I was her puppet to play with. The supposed proof that her system of being the perfect woman really worked. She was angling to get a book deal, then end up on talk shows."

He slipped an arm around me, cuddling me against his shoulder. "I'm so sorry, baby. Knowing that, I'm even more convinced that my plan will work."

"I'm not going out in public tonight." My head rested against his shoulder.

Hawk heaved a dramatic sigh, then turned to face me head on, placing his finger under my chin. "If you don't come with me tonight, I'm going to contact your mother and tell her exactly what you saw when we first met."

"You wouldn't." A giggle bubbled out of me, but he remained serious.

"I absolutely would. Hell, I'll send photos. I'll tell her that you're living with a man, and love taking bubble baths in front of me."

"Hawk, I appreciate your sense of humor, but I—"

He gently clapped a hand over my mouth. "Look, this is the last time I'm going to play the man of the house card, but it's important. Come to this party with me. If it doesn't work, I will help you move anywhere you want."

"You don't have that kind of money," I muttered against his palm.

"Yes I do," he said, raising an eyebrow. "And as soon as you're dressed, I'll explain."

16

HAWK

Lila knew that I was just teasing about sending her Mom a dick pic, but at least it got her butt in gear.

Half an hour later I was nervously pacing when she came out of her room. An odd choking sound got caught in my throat, and I had to clear it before I could speak. "Lila, you look stunning."

The dove gray dress was just low-cut enough to hint at a whisper of cleavage, and long enough that it almost grazed her knees. I'd given the dress shop lady a detailed rundown of everything on Genevieve Astor's blog about what proper ladies wear to wedding-related social events.

Her charcoal high heels showed off her lovely sculpted calves, silver jewelry completed the understated look, and Lila had done some magic with gray and brown eyeshadow that made her indigo eyes glow.

She did a slow twirl, then stopped in front of me. "You're really going to make me do this?"

Taking her hand, I said, "I know that you're scared. I could explain everything to you now, and you could be nervous on the entire ride there. Or, you can trust me, and

I'll tell you what's going on just as we're walking in. Which would you prefer?"

She shook her head, sending her glossy black hair spilling around her shoulders. Then she sighed. "How long of a drive is it?"

"About half an hour. It's on the north edge of the city."

Lila nodded decisively. "I'm better off not knowing yet."

We went downstairs, and her eyes grew wide as she saw the gleaming town car and driver waiting. "I'll explain in about twenty-eight minutes," I said, helping her into the back seat.

As we drove, I could feel the wall go up between us. The bond was broken. Our closeness had a gaping hole in it.

Lila was drawing away, and getting ready to run again. I couldn't let that happen, couldn't let the love of my life disappear.

My only hope was that she might share my sense of adventure. That in her heart, she was the kind of person who wanted to stick it to the man.

Except this time "the man" was her mother.

17

LILA

"After we're announced, I won't be touching you, other than taking your arm, unless we're dancing," Hawk said.

My eyes rolled automatically. "Sounds like you've been talking to my mother."

"No. I've been studying her blog," he explained.

I blinked in surprise. "Really?"

"Yes. Did you know, for example, that once a couple are officially together, it is the man's decision where they should live? Well, I decide that we should live anywhere you like." His smirk was both sexy and adorable. "I'm going to weaponize every stupid declaration she's made on that blog, and we are going to use it to our advantage."

The car pulled into a lavish country club, and Hawk slipped out first, then offered his hand.

Although my heart leapt from his touch, it sank again from the reality of what was happening. "All of that crap only applies if you're in the circles she approves of," I said sadly.

Hawk's eyes blazed as his mouth dipped to my ear.

"Baby, I'm Michael Kingston. As in the Fernbrook Kingstons."

My mouth fell open in shock for a full ten seconds, then my gasp made him chuckle. "That means your mother...is Doris Ashby-Kingston?"

"That's her. The woman your mother deems to be 'the highest authority in matters of style and taste'. So I assume that I'm...worthy?"

My head was spinning. Doris Ashby-Kingston was several steps higher than Mom on her bizarre social ladder. She'd been dying to create ways even to meet the woman.

"If the doorman weren't staring at us, I would kiss you right now," I whispered. "Then I would slap you. How could you keep something like that from me?"

His gorgeous eyes softened. "After you expressed such contempt for that world, I was afraid to tell you. Everything between us was going so fast. I didn't know if you could take that bit of information quite yet."

His hand slipped around my waist. "Even though you took another bit of...*information*...from me quite well. And will again tonight, if I'm lucky."

Giggling, I turned my head so that the doorman couldn't see my cheeks flaming. "You can't say things like that," I whispered.

"You love it," he said. "You love that I'm your filthy, uncontrollable man."

"Maybe a bit," I said, pulling myself together.

A screech of tires snapped our attention to the long driveway, where a bright green sports car had just pulled a clumsy turn toward us.

Hawk's lips grazed my ear. "I love you, Lila. You're the only woman I would do this for. It's going to be spectacular."

Before I could respond, he took my arm and marched us

inside, straight into the world of exquisite marble floors, grand crystal chandeliers, and constant prying eyes.

All the stuffy, traditional garbage that made me slightly queasy. Yet this time it was temporary, and on our terms.

As our names were announced and we entered the room, I was filled with a strange sense of calm. Hawk knew this world, and seemed comfortable in it. He could take control. Which he did as we circled the room, expertly greeting people we had barely heard of as if they were old friends.

When we finally managed to grab a glass of champagne and retreat to a corner, Hawk grinned. "You're a natural at this. I'm sorry, I know that's not what you want to hear."

Leaning closer, I whispered, "It actually wasn't even my best work. I'm a bit distracted. "

"Really?" he grinned, licking his lips. "By what?"

Looking straight into his eyes, I murmured, "I was wondering whether it would feel better if I was on top tonight, or maybe if I should bend over the back of the couch and you could take me from behind."

Hawk choked a sputtering laugh, then he took a sip of champagne while shaking his head. "Damn, baby."

"What's wrong?" I asked innocently. "You don't like it when I tease you back?"

He reached out to trace a finger surreptitiously down my spine. "I think you know how much I like it."

I felt, rather than saw, a shadow beside us, and spun my head to see Gerald approaching. My brother and I had never gotten along, but I saw the relief in his eyes as he realized it was really me.

After introducing him to Hawk, or rather, Michael, it was strange to see Gerald deferring to the older man.

"Mother is going to be so excited to hear about you two,"

Gerald smiled with his forced fake sweetness. "She'll want to have you for dinner as soon as possible."

He gave me a pointed look. "Which means that she's going to require your new phone number."

Hawk recited his email. "Lila and I are doing a low technology experiment," he said. "No cell phones for a month, and we only check my email once a day. Apparently it's good for clearing your mind."

Wow, he really had read Mom's blog. She was always going on about challenges to better oneself. Although she loved email, she detested the immediacy of cell phones. To her, email was far more formal and therefore appropriate.

"Perfect," Gerald said. "I'm sure she'll want to have you both to the house this weekend. "

"Oh, I'm afraid we're out of town this weekend," Hawk said smoothly. "But I think we're free next weekend, aren't we, Lila?"

"I believe so." It was very sweet of him to give me some extra time to wrap my mind around what was happening.

"If you'll excuse me," Gerald said, "some dear friends just arrived."

The second he left, Hawk's arm slid around my waist for a tiny hug. "Is that okay, baby? Dinner with your folks once in a while, my folks once in a blue moon, and we'll basically be free of them."

My giant sigh of relief made him flash that handsome grin. "You're brilliant," I said. "I know I shouldn't say that because it's going to go directly to your head."

"Or somewhere else." His eyebrows went up and down suggestively.

"Oh my God, stop it," I smirked, setting my empty champagne glass aside. "I think it's time for us to do one dance in front of the event photographer, then call it a night."

After barely touching Hawk for the past hour, not to mention the past few days, his arms around me felt incredible. Our dancing was polite enough not to cause a scene, but Hawk teased me by tickling and groping me slightly whenever we were spinning too fast for anyone to notice, although he behaved himself whenever the photographer had his lens trained on us.

At the end of the song he held me close, pressing his erection against my belly. "I don't know if I can wait till we get home," he growled in my ear. "Seeing this elegant, proper side of you makes me need to strip you naked and have my wicked way with you immediately."

"Never trust the help to keep a secret," I said, imitating my mother's nasal voice. "We will not behave in such a fashion in front of your driver."

Hawk pouted, making me laugh a bit too loudly. "Let's go," he said, taking my arm and ushering us to the door.

It was going to take all of my willpower to keep our clothing on during the drive.

18

HAWK

After kissing each other during the entire drive home, I barely made it through the door of our apartment before pulling Lila's dress up over her head. Her glossy dark hair fanned around her as she laughed, pulling off my jacket and tie.

"Sweet Jesus," I breathed, staring at her slender but curvy figure barely covered by silver gray lingerie.

"A lady must dress correctly from the inside out," she said.

I threw my shirt aside, then led us into my bedroom. "My lady is breathtaking." My hands slipped around her back to unfasten her bra, letting her tip forward so she could shake it off.

Tossing it behind me, I wrapped my lips around one pretty pink nipple, then the other. Lila leaned back into my palm pressed against her shoulder blades. My other hand dropped to slip inside her panties, which were drenched. Sliding my fingers through her wet pussy lips, her soft moans made my cock positively throb with need.

My middle finger glided inside so easily I almost didn't

realize I was doing it. Lila's legs began to tremble, so I lifted her to the bed and pulled her panties slowly down her legs.

"If you keep squirming your hips like that, I can't be held responsible for my actions," I said sternly.

"Okay," she breathed, spreading her legs wide for me. I loved seeing her so frantic from desire.

As my palms skimmed up her inner thighs, her soft body trembled. The first lick of my tongue through her pussy triggered a sobbing, choked sound and Lila's fingers grabbed onto my hair.

The taste of her sweet juices was too much. Reaching down to quickly unfasten my belt and pants, I had to give my dick some breathing room.

Encouraging a proper young lady to give in to physical desire to the point where she couldn't see straight anymore was wildly satisfying. My finger slipped into her soaking pussy slowly, teasingly, moving in and out.

"Tell me what you need, Lila," I breathed across her silky skin.

She hesitated only a second, then whispered, "Your tongue. Please."

I was impressed that she spoke up right away. "Good," I murmured as the tip of my tongue swirled around her swollen, needy clit. "I want you to always tell me what you need, baby."

Fluttering my tongue, I waited until I could feel the tension building, feel her legs begin to clamp around me. Then I switched to sharp upward strokes, flattening my entire tongue as I ran it across the surface of her hot little button.

Her breath sounded ragged, nearly painful as she moaned. My tongue and finger became more forceful, controlling her pleasure as she began to twitch.

I'd never felt so deeply connected with anyone or anything. Her pleasure was my pleasure. I was completely tuned in to every breath, every trembling flutter. Turning my palm up, I added a second finger, finding her g-spot and rubbing against it as I licked harder and faster.

Lila made a strange hoarse sound, then her spine curled up as she stared wide-eyed, shaking as deep tremors ran through her. When she collapsed back onto the bed, I lapped up her juices, then kissed her inner thigh down to her knee.

I stood up and grinned down at her. "I hope that my little woman likes to do laundry. If you keep making a mess like this all over my sheets, it's going to be your job."

Lila's light laugh stopped the second my pants hit the floor. Stripping completely, I lay beside her on the bed.

My cock was so hard my stomach muscles were straining. The pressure was so intense that I wondered if my reaction to Lila would ever calm down. Every single second that we were together was creating a new memory that burned into my soul.

"You make me so hot, baby," I murmured against her lips, pulling our bodies together until it felt like every inch of skin possible was touching.

She squirmed gently, pressing her breasts against my pecs. "I can't believe what you do to me," she whispered.

"Tell me about it," I groaned, throwing her leg around my hip as I pulled us closer.

She took my length in her hand and stroked her pussy with it, wetting my skin with her juices. "I would never have been able to do something like this before," Lila smiled sweetly.

"Because it's improper, or because you're shy?"

"Both."

Fisting the back of her hair, I kissed her deeply, possessively, as the tip of my cock parted her wet pussy lips.

"Not anymore," I rasped. "You can't be shy around me. Just open, and honest, and as horny as you want."

"And as soon as my mother formally approves of you, I'll be allowed to kiss you," she laughed.

"You're never going to give a single fuck what she thinks again," I growled, easing my length inside her. "It's just you and me, baby. We belong together. I'm going to spoil you rotten with my love until you can't take it anymore."

Lila's pretty lips fell open as she gasped, "Hawk."

She was the only woman who really knew the real me. I was the only man who truly knew her.

And I already knew it would be this way for the rest of our lives.

19

LILA

Hawk's body entering mine was so much more than sex. It was a declaration that we were together. We were one. Forever.

"I forgot to tell you something," I managed to whisper while trying to breathe. It was slightly uncomfortable as he stretched me wide, but felt incredible.

"What's that?"

His eyes locked on mine as I whispered, "I love you, too."

Those perfect lips grazed mine in the sweetest kiss. "I love you, baby. I love you so much that I'm not even going to make a crack about what part of me you fell in love with first."

My hand swatted his ass, then caressed it as he plunged deeper.

"I love that you're so wet for me," he groaned. "You're so gorgeous, inside and out."

My sexy sweet man was opening me up, possessing me, making me his. The tension in his eyes told me he was trying to control his movements, trying to be gentle.

Hawk caressed my breasts, my hip, easing himself

deeper as he kissed me gently. Finally he buried his cock completely inside me, his long, slow strokes brushing every single nerve. It felt like my pussy was tightening around him, squeezing in time with my heartbeat.

He gripped my hip harder, rocking us together as his teeth tugged at my earlobe. "I've never thought that I deserved anything special. But now that I have you, the most breathtaking woman on Earth, I'm never letting go."

I didn't want to come so fast, but there was no stopping the pleasure flooding my entire body.

"Yes," he murmured, capturing my lips as I came in deep waves, squeezing and tightening around him.

As soon as I stopped trembling, he pulled his length out and froze, breathing deeply. "You feel too good," he said after a moment.

After he caught his breath, he eased just the head inside me again. My pussy was now so sensitive from the incredible climax that I shivered hard.

"Too much?" he asked.

"Almost."

He grinned, kissing my forehead. "Then I guess you wouldn't want me to do this?" He thrust inside me with one quick stroke, making me cry out. "Or this?" He did it again, then again, until I couldn't stop shaking.

It was overwhelming. It was everything. I never wanted it to stop.

I whined as he pulled out, sitting up on his knees. Then he lifted me back onto his shaft, keeping his hands under my ass so he could bounce me up and down.

"Hold onto my neck, baby."

I held us together as we kissed awkwardly but desperately while I moved up and down on his cock. The inner walls of my sex started to clench again. Hawk groaned, then wrapped his arm around me so that he could use his free hand to brush his thumb against my clit.

"Oh God, yes," I gasped against his lips. I couldn't believe how deeply he was thrusting inside me. I felt the pressure all the way up my abdomen.

"It feels like you like this, baby. Or maybe I should stop?"

"Don't you dare," I gasped. My hips were rocking against him, pulling him even deeper as the pace increased.

"Do you want more?" I loved the way he spoke against my lips, as if he couldn't bear to end our kiss to talk.

"Yes," I gasped, listening to the filthy, wet sound of our bodies slapping together harder.

His thumb pressed into my clit, fluttering while increasing the pressure. He slammed into me harder, lifting me with every stroke as a much larger orgasm hovered, waiting to break free.

"Squeeze me, baby," he growled, his eyes half lidded with lust as we moved together. "Show me that you want me to come deep inside you."

"Yes," I choked, then I screamed as the climax tore through me, releasing every drop of tension as I squirmed and shook.

"Damn, girl," he grit out, as I felt his huge cock swelling inside me. His raspy growl took over as he pounded harder, deeper, filling me with bursts of his seed.

"I love you." Still thrusting up into me, his lips peppered my face with kisses. "I love you, Lila."

"I love you, Hawk."

My fingers gripped his shoulders as we finally stilled. "Unless you expect me to call you Michael now?"

"Almost never," he said with a grin. "But you can call me anything you want." He held my hand, kissing my knuckles as we laid down. "I'm yours, and as long as you're calling me something every single day, I'm the luckiest man alive."

"I'm the lucky one," I laughed, snuggling under his arm. "You're the perfect blend of rebel and upstanding society man."

"Don't forget the best part of all," he said, raising one eyebrow.

I pursed my lips. "The next words from your mouth had better be PG-rated, mister."

He gasped in mock surprise. "I was going to mention my fabulous cooking skills, not my dick, thank you very much."

I'd never laughed with anyone so much in my life. Even more proof that we belonged together, and that our new life was going to be happy and relaxed. Two things that I'd never really had the courage to dream of for myself before.

Somehow, this strange man had made all of my wishes come true, even though he didn't really know what they were yet.

And we were going to spend the rest of our lives making up new dreams to fulfill together.

EPILOGUE ONE
HAWK ~ SEVEN MONTHS LATER

As we walked up the stairs to our apartment, Lila asked, "Are you okay? You've been a bit quiet."

"Yeah, baby. I'm fine."

I kissed the top of her head then unlocked the door. "Just a busy day," I said. "Oh – and the realtor called. She has a bunch of listings for us to go over to start thinking about what sort of house we'd like."

"Amazing." Lila's perky smile flooded my chest with the familiar warm glow. My sweet girl always filled me with joy, but two weeks ago, when she said she was ready for us to buy a house, she made me the happiest man in the world.

Now, I was about to seriously push my luck. Lila had her own ideas about traditions, and what was proper. She loved some traditions, and didn't think much of others. So it was tricky to gauge what her reaction would be to this.

"You said that we're going out for dinner Friday night, right?" she asked.

"Yes. I'm going to need you to wear that dark blue dress, please."

Leading Lila to the living room, I sat down on the couch and pulled her close beside me.

"If we're going out for a fancy dinner Friday, can we just order pizza tonight?" she asked.

"Sure. But first I wanted to get your opinion on something."

She gave a heavy sigh, rolling her eyes. "Thank goodness. Out with it. You've been weird tonight."

Damn. She'd picked up on how nervous I was.

Lila stroked my cheek, smiling sweetly. "Let me guess. Do you want to wait a bit longer to buy a house? I'm fine with that, if you want to take some more time..."

"Oh my God – no." I clutched her hand, kissing the back of it. "No, baby. I want to buy a house with you the second you choose the right one."

"You're sure?" Her eyebrows raised in that sassy way that said she wasn't one hundred percent sure I was telling the truth.

"Absolutely. I've known you're the woman for me from the first time you stared at my—"

As always, her hand clapped across my mouth. "Are you ever going to stop mentioning that?"

She giggled at my muffled, "Nope. Never."

I took her hand and slipped it down my chest, pressing against my t-shirt so that she felt a crinkle of plastic. "What's that?"

"I'll show you in a minute."

Dragging her hand down my chest suggestively, I took a detour at the top of my jeans, bringing her fingers to a small box in my pocket.

Standing up, I pulled it out and snapped it open quickly before she might think it was a ring.

Lila gasped, her fingers trailing along the earrings. The

one carat round indigo sapphires were encircled with tiny white diamonds.

"It was tricky to find stones dark enough that almost match your eyes," I said. "I wanted to get you something special, but not so fancy you couldn't wear them every day if you wanted to."

"They are stunning," she breathed. Her fingers were trembling, which made me think I'd better hurry and get to my main point.

"Your eyes are the most beautiful thing in this world," I said softly. "I've drawn so many women for tattoos over the years, and my dream women have always looked like you."

Lila put the earrings on, giving me her adorably shy smile. "That's really sweet, Hawk."

"I'd get a portrait of you tattooed on me, if it wasn't such bad luck," I said.

"I know that even getting someone's name is bad luck," she said. "So I hope you never do that."

"Are you saying that you want us to be together forever?"

"Yes."

"Good."

I pulled off my shirt, loving the way her tongue darted across her lips. But then her eyes locked on the bandage on my chest just left of center. Peeling it up from the bottom, I showed her the fresh tattoo of a round deep blue sapphire.

"It took Lars and I quite a while to figure out how to layer the colors so that it looked 3-D," I said. "Basically, I wanted a tattoo that represents you, while being abstract enough to not be bad luck. You know what I mean?"

Lila stared, unblinking. Then as soon as her eyelids flickered, a single tear slipped down her cheek. "It's beautiful," she breathed. "You really got that for me? A mark over your heart?"

"Yes." Sliding off the couch so that I was on my knees, I held her hands.

"I know that you get overwhelmed easily, baby, so I'm sort of doing this backwards. Tomorrow we're going shopping to get you an incredible engagement ring. I didn't want to risk getting one that wasn't something you loved."

Lila was already nodding as I said, "You know I adore you with all my heart, baby. Friday night at dinner, when I offer you the ring and ask you to marry me, are you going to say yes?"

Her chin tipped up and down even faster.

"I'm following all of your mother's rules on Friday. A formal venue, and a photographer at a discreet distance to capture the moment. But tonight is just for us. I need you to know how much you mean to me, Lila. You're my darling girl, and I can't imagine living without you, whether it's in a weird warehouse loft apartment, or a house, or anywhere else on this planet."

Kissing her hands gently, I was touched at how bravely she fought to hold back her tears.

"I love you, baby. Will you marry me?"

"Yes," she sniffled, blinking away tears. "Even without the ring, or the dinner, or Mom's approval."

"I appreciate that. But we're going to do it right."

"I love you so much," she breathed, wrapping her arms around the back of my neck. "I love how you make things acceptable to our families and still make everything feel like us."

"All we have to do is play their game now and then." I held her close, stroking her back gently. "It'll be a lot easier in the long run. Plus, our mothers will basically take care of the entire wedding, right?"

More tears slipped down Lila's face as she began to

laugh. "Excellent point." She steadied herself with a deep breath before whispering, "I love you so much, Hawk."

"I love you, Lila."

I wanted to tell her that I knew we belonged together forever. But it felt more important to simply hold her in my arms while her tears of joy dripped onto my chest, just missing the fresh tattoo over my heart that was the precise color of her eyes when she was happy.

EPILOGUE TWO
LILA ~ EIGHT YEARS LATER

Flattening myself against the wall of the hallway, I barely inched my face around the corner to peek into the living room. I knew better than to interrupt daddy-daughter time.

The girls seemed to have three different personalities. They were creative and smart and communicative with me. When Hawk and I were together, they were pretty well balanced. But when Hawk had them alone, my sweet little girls became fearless, and tried to prove to him how tough they were.

"You can do it, Cara," our four-year-old Gemma encouraged. "Do it like this."

She demonstrated for her eleven-month old sister by sitting in front of her, then using the couch cushions to pull herself up to standing. Then Gemma showed how to grip the edges of the couch to stay balanced as she walked over to her dad.

"Good idea, Gemma," Hawk said, ruffling her hair.

Cara loved having her hair played with, so that was the last straw. She shimmied her little diapered butt closer to the couch, then I stared in disbelief as her tiny fingers gripped the cushions.

She had only learned to crawl properly last month, having discovered that Hawk would wait on her hand and foot if she gave him a certain smile.

He caught my eye, giving me an excited nod as we stared at our baby pulling herself up to standing. Cara took a moment to get her balance, then sidestepped to the right, holding the cushions for dear life.

"You're doing it!" Gemma squealed, clapping her hands in glee. She stepped back so that Cara could make her way over to Daddy, then grip the knees of his jeans as she continued on.

He ruffled her hair, which made her giggle. I thought that she'd stop there, but instead she used first the coffee table, then the easy chair, and lastly the bookcase to keep on going.

Hawk looked over again and blew me a kiss. It was yet another perfect moment in our wonderful, amazing lives.

My sweet husband had been the perfect man for me from the very beginning.

Even when he surprised me by having our parents hiding across from the restaurant when he proposed. Even when he shocked me by stretching our week-long honeymoon in Europe to a month. Our mothers arranged it all, after planning our wedding.

He was able to leverage their strengths and channel their pushy mother energy while keeping them at enough of a distance that I didn't feel smothered. Somehow he was always able to find the perfect balance.

Tearing my eyes away from my handsome man, I looked down to see Cara precariously balanced on her toes, looking in all directions, wondering where to go next. There was nothing else for her to grab onto.

Stepping out of the hallway, I dropped to my knees and held out my arms. "Come here, sweetie," I said gently, hoping not to startle her.

Somehow the surprise made her forget that she didn't have any support, and she awkwardly toddled three feet across the carpet and into my embrace.

Gemma was beside herself, jumping and clapping. Hawk scooped her up in his arms as I picked up Cara, and we met in the middle of the room for a big family hug.

"Cara wants pizza for dinner," Gemma announced, employing her usual trick to try to get anything she wanted.

Hawk raised an eyebrow, looking at her sternly. "Pizza is only for nice girls who show their sister how to tidy up the play corner."

"Okay!"

We set the kids down so that Gemma could run to the corner to start pitching toys into baskets, while Cara crawled after her to watch.

Hawk slipped an arm around my waist and whispered, "I ordered the pizza ten minutes ago." He nuzzled my ear, as his hands gripped my hip suggestively. "And tonight for dessert, we can have another slice of what we started after my shower this morning."

"Maybe," I said, stretching up to kiss him. "Or maybe two."

Not only was he the perfect husband, my sexy man was still the perfect roommate...who still loved coming out of the shower buck naked just to tease me.

∾

RELATED STORIES

Meet Lila's roommate Ashley in
HER NEW BODYGUARD: JACKSON

~

Excerpt:

A tall shadow came toward me. "Well done, Ashley."

It was the same deep voice from the phone call. He stepped into the dim glow of the single lightbulb over us. "Pleased to meet you. I'm Jackson."

Holy crap. The man was gorgeous. And huge. *Wow.* I would have been afraid of him if I met him in a dark alley and he hadn't just saved me from some unknown stalker. There was a faint scar along his temple that made him even sexier.

As he held out his hand to shake mine, I was still fluttering like a leaf. He took both of my hands, then led me over to two battered lawn chairs near a workbench in the far corner.

"It's okay," he said, drawing the chairs closer together and sitting us down. "It's over. Just breathe."

There was something about him holding my hands that made me flutter in a way that had nothing to do with fear. The man was breathtaking. Absolutely striking deep brown eyes bored into mine as he smiled gently.

"I'm so sorry I was called into this job at the last second, and wasn't able to pick you up in the city," he said. "You did wonderfully, though. So many people panic, instead of following simple directions."

"I'm pretty sure I did a bit of both." We both heard my voice hitch.

His left hand still held mine, as the right reached out to lightly caress the back of my shoulder. "We got the job done," he said with a warm smile. "That's all that matters for now."

After a few deep breaths, my heart was no longer racing from panic adrenaline, but it was definitely pounding from the way he was touching me. Even though he was simply comforting me in a very appropriate way, I'd never been so near to such an incredible looking man before. It made my stomach tighten and churn.

"You seem to know everything about me. Who are you?" I asked.

His smile grew slightly. "Jackson Bradshaw. Your new bodyguard. I've been assigned to keep you safe, isolated, and on the move if necessary for the next forty-eight hours."

∾

Meet Lila's downstairs neighbor Dana in
  MR. RIGHT... ON TIME

~

Excerpt:

To change your energy, change your hair.

To change your whole life, change your city. Simple.

That's what I did a few years ago. First, I put perky purple streaks in my super-light blonde, shoulder-length shag. It might be silly, but they made me feel like I could avoid being officially grown up for a little bit longer.

Then I ran away to find myself, or whatever pop psychology books were calling it back then. I read them all, but the underlying vibe was always the same: listen to your heart.

I did that for three years, crisscrossing the country with touring indie bands. Now, though, it was time to feel grounded. I wanted to turn my loft apartment into my dream home, and hopefully find a truly nice guy...in a few years. For the moment my eyes were open for someone hot and fun.

Hoping to invite male energy into my life, last night I added teal streaks to my hair along with the purple for a fun change.

I hummed to myself while grinding another batch of coffee beans. A barista at the café inside the city's best bookstore was the perfect job for now.

Wiping my hands on my apron, I started speaking my opening line before I'd even turned toward the counter. "Good morning, sunshine, what can I get you?"

As I focussed, the most stunning sapphire blue eyes came into view. "Whatever you'd recommend for someone running on two hours of sleep with a crucial meeting in an hour."

The breath was knocked out of me. He was gorgeous.

Like...model gorgeous. And dressed so well he could be on the cover of one of those fancy men's clothing magazines.

I felt the urge to try to impress him. But I also wanted to help out someone who was having a rough time at work. Heaven knows, I knew what being underslept felt like.

Whirling around, I pulled three shots of espresso. I handed him the first one in a china cup. "Slam that," I commanded. Then I fixed an Americano in a to-go cup with the other two shots. I also handed him a bag with three protein balls.

"Wait ten minutes, then sip the Americano slowly," I said. "Don't let the caffeine peak until after your meeting. The protein balls are to fight exhaustion. Also, hydrate." I reached for a bottle of water, but he waved me off.

"I have a water bottle in my car. Thank you, Dana."

He swiped his bank card as I stared up at him in surprise. Most of the businesspeople didn't take the time to read my name tag. I always assumed I was invisible to them.

"I really appreciate this," he said. He started to leave, then turned back with a grin and a saucy wink. "I like the new teal bits, by the way."

He hurried out the door, leaving me staring at his fit, muscular frame and positively stunning ass. The dark suit pants fit perfectly.

Why would a man like that notice and remember me? And why was my heart racing as if I'd just met a movie star?

～

SHACKED UP LOVE - SERIES

This Summer some of your favorite authors have come together to bring you a new series all about falling in love with your roommate. As the temperatures rise outside, things are getting even steamier in the close quarters of their apartments!

Protected By My Roommate - Cameron Hart

Faking it with my Roommate - Khloe Summer

Tempted by my Roommate - Shaw Hart

Stalked by my Roommate - Matilda Martel

Intoxicated by my Roommate - Chelsea MacDonald

Pregnant by my Roommate - Violet Rae

Schooled by my Roommate - Piper Cook

Screwed by my Roommate - Heather Dahlgren

Teased by my Roommate - Haley Travis

Bossed by my Roommate - Penn Rivers

Kissed by my Roommate - Ember Davis

Dared by my Roommate - Cassie Mint

Owned by my Roommate - Imani Jay

Hated by my Roommate - Logan Chance

ALSO BY HALEY TRAVIS

Never Date The Boss

Ashley was talked into one little "business date" with her boss, and everything changed in a heartbeat. Or rather, a flutter of them.

Mr. Right... As Rain

A gorgeous man saved me on the way to an interview. Maybe it was the good luck kiss from a stranger, but I got both the job and an instant boyfriend. Isn't falling in love so fast just a fantasy?

Daddy's Billionaire Boss

When Emily discovers her Dad's boss is the improbable man her aunt predicted she'd fall for, can she fit into his world?

Scrappily Ever After

Finding love through a new book club, a scrap of paper, a little blood, and telling time in cups of tea.

Please join the mailing list: haleytravisromance.com for new releases, updates, discounts & freebies! Search @haleytravisromance on social media.